What's That Noise?

By William Carman

Random House 🏠 New York

What's that noise?

Are the neighbors
mowing the lawn?

Could there be a monster
in my closet?

It better not be an octopus
in the bathtub.

I hear it in the hall.

It sounds like a bear
in Mom and Dad's bedroom.

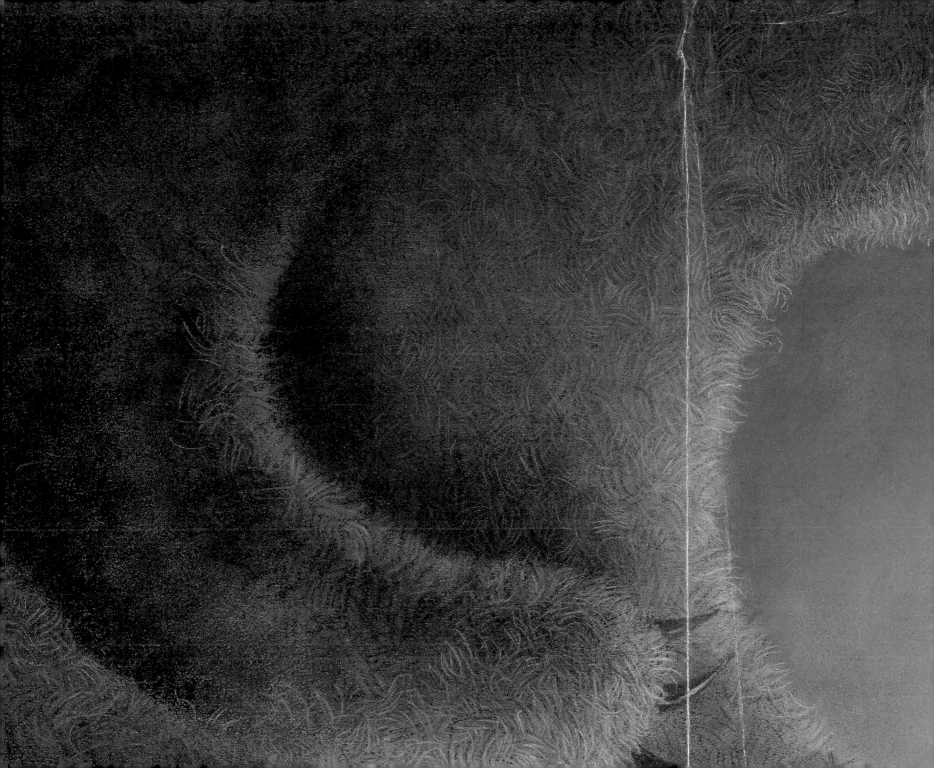

I've got to warn them!

For M and M—B.C.

Copyright © 2002 by William Carman. All rights reserved under International and
Pan-American Copyright Conventions. Published in the United States by Random House, Inc.,
New York, and simultaneously in Canada by Random House of Canada Limited, Toronto.

www.randomhouse.com/kids

Library of Congress Cataloging-in-Publication Data
Carman, William.
What's that noise? / by William Carman.
p.   cm.
Summary: A boy hears a noise in the night and imagines what it could be.
ISBN 0-375-81052-8 (trade) — ISBN 0-375-91052-2 (lib. bdg.)
[1. Sound—Fiction. 2. Imagination—Fiction. 3. Night—Fiction.] I. Title.
PZ7.C21695 Wh 2002
[E]—dc21
00-059106

Printed in the United States of America First Edition July 2002 10 9 8 7 6 5 4 3 2 1

RANDOM HOUSE and colophon are registered trademarks of Random House, Inc.